U

J. R. ORTIZ

TO BE ALL
IN ALL
FOR ALL

Table of Contents

Blood Rose
In Movements of the Sea
Sea at Night
Circumference of the Earth
Adrift
Loving You
Free Tree Grows
Meditations on a Cloud
As Only This Life Escapes Me
Act I   Sea
Mighty World
Search for Immortality
Passage of Time
Eyes of Defiance
Tremble of the Night
We Were Children, Once
Dystopia
A Walk Through Trees
Animalization of Man
Act II   Land
Impermanence of Permanence
You
The Struggle
Strong Man Son
If I Had Not Known You
Absence and Persistence
The Night We Met
Grand Salvador
On Your Birthday
Act III   Air
Acknowledgements

Blood Rose

In carmine vein flows of holy blood rose,
at stops and gates of red oneiric anastomose -
love waits thru both angry and tender life blows...
The mixed mind woes of fire spirit – I suppose;
soft velvet petal, sharp thorn - eternal prose...

Into welcome innocent sea, I pass;
sacred flower clutched tight in hand.
Away! Away from crazed humanity mass,
from homeland to unknown dreamland.

Refugee from rich bannered history,
past heroes and honored freedom;
a mad escape from birth country,
lost liberty and forgotten martyrdom.

Sail on alone to new hopes offshore,
in search endeavor to breathe free.
With hard oar and roar – to new lore;
inside, with all lessons taught to me.

The good voice is strong –
like echo song whispered into eternity;
to guide and remind for long –
an urge for sanity and soul prosperity.

No looking back - the dear past is golden past.
Onward and forward, my rapid story goes.
In loving remembrance, I remain steadfast;
and hold hand to heart, with treasured blood rose.

In Movements of the Sea

In movements of proud open sea,
in rush and sway of deep blue and grey;
in all mind and clear eye, in all beauty be;
in all thoughts on brisk and steely day...

Great rise, great fall, white white froth of wave;
salt and haze shimmer light in warm moist air;
colored rings around Saturn sun, burst out rave;
lost far away horizon, fast raging storm from there...

Menace wind and wicked tower water spout,
Neptune's good angels and rigid devils fight it out.
Am only an innocent rider of mad last tempest.
Must arrive brave – alive, avoid near death pressed...

Be still my heart! Brace mind and body!
Swift return to me! Fill weary soul with tenacity!
Image now clear, amongst grand disturbance here.
Your fine love and peace serene, calm quiet the fear...

Oh - dear fond enamored girl, strong furnace within me!
Envelop and fuse into total spirit, our complete sanctity!
In dark blinding tornadoes of ocean Earth, I still see –
your eyes, your smile, your heart – in all angry ferocity...

Sea at Night

One alone, on sea at night -
dark dark black water, low starlight;
blue bioluminescence, moon bright;
blurred eye view, but strong mind sight.

Singing siren wind, loud lapping wave;
no land seen, only far distant ships.
Shout out angry rave, with voice God gave;
weak bloodied body, parched mouth and lips.

No call return… I sit and wait and learn.
Exiled away from Motherland and family.
Dead tired, soul and heart in hurt burn;
absent my love, searching for remedy.

On my back in black, under Milky Way;
faded white gaseous suns and nebulae.
Ready for what comes, and all that may;
take deep breath, expire silent sigh…

Hand pass thru phosphorescent water glow;
churn sky and sea, grand bioluminescent flow.
Banding stirs of plankton on marine canvas below;
God's fantastic Earth in a wild cobalt show indigo.

I'd wish to be like Perseus on Pegasus,
coyote spirit stealing fire from heavens.
No fear here, in strong perilous emphasis –
Grasp elusive courage, all truth beckons.

Toward Andromeda, I speed sail,
to save nude nymph from Poseidon's beast.

A pure mission just, I must not fail;
from cruel chains, I'll free – released...

Circumference of the Earth

Along meridian equator, Earth's circum of 25,000 miles;
great ball spinning on axis like a top, thousand miles per
hour.
My eyes in morning seek eastern sun, tribulations and
trials -
to sense the awesome speed power, meditative trance
tower...

A circular orbit tour around brilliant yellow blinding
central star,
rushing rapid at 67,000 miles per life hour in short year
complete.
With Mars and Venus, and neighbor planets, we go fast
and far.
Grand holy hot cosmic field - nothing appears small,
nothing petite.

On small outer arm spur of our milky path galaxy, my
Earth sits;
never still, but racing half million miles per hour around
black hole.
Star billions in God symphony spiral fly, in furious stellar
magic blitz.
A super massive light roll - we live in shining shaking
cosmic atoll.

Rotating swath of gas and solid dust ballet into baby star
formation,
adding to community white disk - 100,000 light-years
across...
Milky Way exploding out million miles per hour in universe
inflation -

further and further into the nothing dark, into creation
separation loss…

Am I in my mind, or outside of it?
Nature's gladiator pit, or heavy fever fit?

What am I and thee to be,
in this infinite crazy lonely sea?
Less than tiny ants on colossus,
asleep or conscious?

How are we to live in ever misgive,
or exhaustive yearn combative?

Bold!
Bolder!
Boldest!

In bliss and vibrant love, and long free!
You for me…
I for thee…
All heart and soul and energy…

To live evermore,
and forevermore – give…

Adrift

When you have lived and done right, but all future seems
lost;
when black tunnel end is near, and you sense doom and
fear.
Old control of imagined destiny, an ultimate mirage
exhaust;
with now only oblivion frontier, open mouth of the
Acheron clear...

Floating on silent dark purple eternal sea - with no me, no
we;
night sky without color, no calm shine light of moon or
star delight.
Dense obscure opacity, broken rare by cries of far off
banshee.
To hear the wail, as I sail, and be frozen still without sight.

Woeful weeping woman! From what distant tragic land
you howl?
Disrupting my quiet slip unknown! For whom do you
lament?
Do you horror cry from home I come, or is place I go so
too foul?
Do you keen for dead I've seen, or should I consider
myself spent?

No! Stay silent hag! No more whimper scream of reversal
defeat.
Allow me to bob like a cork on sea, and consider the loss
of family.
Let it be! Hush woman! Permit me to browbeat bleak lot I
meet.

Away rapidly! I must gather courage to confront fate in savage gallantry.

So too, I must have time to dream of special girl;
for she is the true and only light in all I vision...
In this demented swirl of life, she is the pearl.
To liberate her, I need all my mental precision...

Alone in darkness now, in solo mind I want to be,
making plans to face my stage and coming apogee...
To fight evil, and rid of chains, to set her soul free.
Kiss gentle, and love her tender - even adrift at sea...

Loving You

Ooooh!
To be lost on infinite sea...
Without strength, without hope – without thee...
Brainy stupor, loose mental images in crazy flight...
Flashes of color beauty, to black and white ugly...
Vivid to eco-strife, and back again to your kind sight.

Hallucinations of cortex, primitive stem now taking
control...
Quickly losing you, a sad dying away of dear memory.
Wish to avoid the abyss hole, raising sword and cross
shield of soul.
Claw and clasp all things YOU, soothing maligned
sensory...

Fields of summer valley come into view, with thirsty
amber and green.
Closed eyes see bright rainbow waves of dancing white
light flowers –
Long file columns of ruby red rose, and others of
cerulean and citrine.
The rolling pass of cooling shade, and rainwater birthing
powers!

Combat with sands of continental desert, rise and fall of
sunburnt silica.
Tall tower dunes in the wind, quartz and coral – a mix of
dead and living;
barren dry vanilla sheets, the hot grain oceans of the
amygdala.
Epitome terrain unforgiving, I search for circle oasis of
water streaming...

Fuel force generator of life, liquid ambrosia – stimulant might of H2O:
in the forest plain and no-man arid clime, a biological full-time need.
For offspring to grow, and all miracle go, the cloud and river must flow.
Grand spread florid Earth, rushing torrid speed germ of sacred seed.

Wild horse quench of water pushes the evolutionary universal drive.
The move forward stride, survive thru every generational era.
Two element magic molecule, for even sleepy almost dead revive alive.
Instrumental since the beginning whirl, and twirls of Amazon and Sahara.

Aquifer demand of unconscious medulla overtakes cerebral reason.
A wanton psychic hunt for ultimate life, testing total spirit treason.
Contest between bio-drive and extreme love drive – a war of conscience.
Water plea and time consume, or die free with thee – that is the substance…

For you are more than mere water to basic instinct lips - all energy drink;
further all body satisfy and gratify, and final assuage for soul senses too.
I think profound of only you, desiring you more than all physical life link.
For you are all, in me all thru, forever and ever – as I lay here, loving you…

Free Tree Grows

From a living cup of fragrant fertile earthy soil and clay,
grows a tiny tiny tree of hope, of love, of ever sunny day.

Young solid bark around shallow woody root and stem,
protects junior vessels of needed water and nutrient
gem.

To strong supply a future wish of plenty luscious verdant
leaf,
and provide kind bounty cover shade in times of sorrow
grief.

Under beauty arc - green grass and wildflower on which
to lay,
and ponder and dream of way for freedom to last and
long stay.

Hold your hand and kiss, and listen silent – gentle wind
blows,
and watch our loving children laugh and play ---
as our free tree grows...

Meditations on a Cloud

Floating on flotsam wood in an endless sea,
cloud above and I in same slow wind flow.
Delirium thoughts, as washed away debris;
too tired to sit and grab oar, and row...

Solar light so strong, my eyes can't bear;
rays reflected from crystal salt on lash.
Beams shot in all direction like rocket flare.
Skin in violent fury, sun burning fry hot flash.

From end to end, blue of bluest sky true;
not a speck of white or grey, except for you.
Big puff of velvet blanch, and pure through;
soft telling forms changing with each view...

Why are you so alone in heaven above me?
Trailing tales, akin to castle parapet sentinel -
from an angel, to Satan and raven imagery,
and back to shapes of my most preferable...

Are you confused in what to represent?
Or is it my mind in world fog, in mixed match?
Are you showing me Truth, or dare invent?
Or are you delirious as I, in mental dispatch?

Ooooh!
Please bring me lovely beauty show...
Of hopeful gentle future with girl I know...
Of fields of white lilies, and Cupid bow...
And of fertile freedom land, I wish to sow...

As Only This Life Escapes Me

I consumed and held hard this life;
devoured all color and light, I recall –
blush of peach, or edged razor knife;
radiant morning rise, calm twilight fall...

As child, I saw and heard more.
I reflected and pondered more.
I clear imagined and sensed more.
Rather sleep – I wished to soar,
and explore...

Words of poetry and song, moved.
Dance ballads and music stir, moved.
Painted canvas and sculpture, moved.
With all art, I fused;
of none, I refused...

As young man, I chased the wind.
Fast and fiery, I never slow crawled.
Hours of day were never long, but trimmed.
The wonder of it all, so enthralled.

Then, the mighty breakthrough day I met you...
All things true prior ceased to be, in explosive finality.
Everything seen, and all soul I past knew,
had been simple formality – forming of personality.

Born into new splendor of sensory pleasure;
where minds and lips and hips mix, and juices flow.
Hearts power together, and eyes see rare treasure.
Eternal energy sparks glow, like few indeed know...

Now, our love amiss...
Dropped into sad absentia, I falter and fade;
no kind hand to hold, no face to kiss, no glee of thee -
no bright hope of great plans made, only tear
cascade...
I long to love you more – our forevermore to be;
central core beat of this heart gone, where passion laid.
I wish to see you at next plateau, by the sea and our
tree.
Be not afraid, my love; please, do not be dismayed...
For I am but one soul with you, always alive and free;
and know all too well of past and present made,
and am certain of future - as only this life escapes me...

ACT I

Sea

From a land raped and burned, and a people turned, I had entered the sea; not to save myself, but to save thee... To the 'Island', I hoped to go – the final refuge.

The last war had come quickly without notice. Society had been forewarned, but remained unsuspecting until the very end. After the atom attacks, our people had gone from civilized conduct to unimaginable savagery.

The 'After War', between numerous large bands of survivors, had further broken down culture. Over seven years, organized tribes formed alliances to vanquish opposing consortiums of competing warriors. In the past months, the 'Blues' and 'Reds' – each composed of thousands of rabid fighting men, women, and children – brutalized each other for control of the main river valley in the south. This region could still produce edible crops, and had the only drinkable water for hundreds of miles. My 'Blues' lost the final battle of the campaign.

Prisoners were not taken in the 'After War'. Genocide was practiced by both sides. Defeat cost thousands of our lives, in battle and its aftermath.

A number of our women and children had escaped to an offshore island. Protected by two hundred young warrior men, our survivor 'Blues' managed to encamp in the safe high hills near the sea. I had been told all this...

On the island, I was sure to find her...

Into the sea, I went; without food or water, or shelter from the sizzling sun and battering wave. With wounds festering, and a confabulating mind deprived of peace, I drifted for days. My wooden float, gathered together from burnt white timber, carried me like Pegasus to my island of hope. Here she would be, I knew...

The missiles had come – the 'End War'...
From teaching prose, I had been drawn.
From reciting beauty, to duty in the 'After War'...
Seven years of killing of every form set upon.

Loss of our homes and loved ones,
our culture and civility thrown to bones.
I had destroyed with knife and axe and guns,
pulverized my fellow Man with sticks and stones.

Our country split in two – the Red and Blue.
An animal primitive combat against ourselves;
the day weaponized, creative heart suffocated too.
Altered men in a fight all reason and logic repels...

To find light in the dimness of infliction,
to release from the physical and psychic pain,
to search for hope and faith without contradiction,

to find some good in the evil human stain...

Where are the decent men among the indecent -
The ones with aspirations to lives with meaning;
those with right of conscience, bold truth recent;
strong holders of humanity eternal flame beaming?

There is no circumstance for injustice!
No allowance for oppression of mind and spirit!
No breakage of natural laws of God's substance!
No reason to feel sharp edge of cutlass, or fear it...

Let us return to our soul's genome.
In our resistance, find the path of right.
Use our deepest sensitivity to write a new tome;
one which lights the dark night to a future bright...

In slow dawn:
after furious black night is gone,
and all energies drawn;
after thought of last breath beneath angry purple wave,
and escape of soul from deepest marine grave;
to see orange sun rise and pacify,
and vivid color of new day free body from do-or-die;
to curl lips in smile of great wonder
and know, if only for a moment under,
that while I'm nearly beaten –
I have life still to give, and sweeten...

Flows of gray and violet sky,
and white purple swirls of ocean foam...
Motions of the beauty Earth belie –
its warring sides and shatter divide dome.

Onto a horizon split of sea from air,

never to touch in bold display.
Shades of blue – yearning fair;
seeking paths of good, truest way...

I could gather no real horizon...
Its disappearance confused me.
From where color bands widen –
the grays, light blue, and aqua be...

Edges of hue defined and clear,
straight lines of bizarre perfection...
Large blocks of unified abstract smear,
eternal end to end Euclid tri-section...

Was the Earth flat, or just my mind?
Would I float off margin blind,
or circle the world, resigned?
What fate before me, so unkind...

The geometrics of the human brain;
the ricochet of thoughts and hopes;
inner works in chain, world of pain;
a circus painted in surreal envelopes...

To where, I sail?
Forever into oceanic bog?
At mercy of calm or gale?
Into God's mathematical analogue?

Before me, a tri-colored picture...
Here in truth, or psychic stricture?
Do I stay in aqua, or move to blue or gray?
Only destiny can judge or say...

So, for now – I will float,

on a sea silent with no direction.
A sea estranged and remote,
and my brain in complete reflection…

I had been a master of my destiny,
always sure knowing where I'd be…
Believing certain of golden fate,
of performing and achieving great…

Forever confident of skill and wisdom,
never doubting success security…
Always a quick answer, a kingdom;
never in obscurity, only of mind purity…

Time tells, future rebels;
twists and switchbacks confound…
Never one for wishing wells,
aware of plans sound…

What torment this tempest brings…
A rock around every bend;
only cold ocean, no warm springs.
No safe tunnels till the end…

I spoke in past of affirmatives,
of truths solid and sure…
Never of the negatives,
or of disease – only the cure…

What to make of this world;
this upside down of you, of me?
With my dreams whirled,
and only answer – "We'll see…"

The indignity of losing one's country and people;

the loss of life, and all other precious things;
to savage barbaric brutes and helpless sheeple;
the endless destruction, and all that brings...

To be lost in outer space of the mind,
frozen stiff in fear and insecurity.
Battle scars taken and given in kind,
forgetting all charity and purity...

Where are we in giant scheme enterprise?
Are there any of us standing, sharp and wise?
To what end we go, left or right?
Do we split in seam, in unjust fight?

Who moves us on human game board?
Philosopher poets, or horde of sword?
Do we listen to rising voices of mad men,
or view sun rise and set - with magic pen?

There is no time remaining...
Sand of hourglass has gone.
There is no allowance for abstaining;
straighten the spine, and wait for new dawn...

In last turn of the screw,
a final tight squeeze freeze...
Determined pursue through,
tease of the expectant ease...

Poisoned world as a nut and bolt;
friction shock of the slow thread.
Ruler on ruled - reversed, steel revolt;
the misled refusing their deathbed...

Grind of the ultimate misplay.
Misguidance astray, all intent to fool...

Setting shop to dismember and flay,
shrink the brain, empty the school...

A final call to Evil, before the Fall...
Recall black raven in dark death view,
and fetid stench of dreaded burial pall...
Stop cold! - Before last turn of the screw.

Surface sea - now glass...
No ripple, even with weak hand pass.
Reflection of face: years of blood struggle,
weak bones, ripped flesh muscle,
wrinkled line furrows of fears,
long tale trails of tears...

I could fall easy into the sea,
sink to muddy bottom internee;
to be picked clean by fishes,
a vicious waste of wishes...

To have been born of Mother,
to this obscene – no serene other.
My color concoctions of mind,
to disappear from Earth of mine...

Emotive feel of old good life track,
compendium stream of all I'd been
as boy and man, to fade in black –
into quick distillate trash bin...

How had I come to this?
Born free, to beastly malady;
hopeful day, to doomed at sea.

In the end, one conjures up all the ifs:
A foggy analysis of twists and turns,

of forks in the road, and forgotten gifts,
of all lessons given, and all the learns...

I have had many fortunes bestowed,
and paid back all my debts owed...
And with all energy remaining,
and soul draining –
I sing my ode...

Sprinting light speed of image memory,
to finish line of grand All-Mighty sensory;
past all the banners and balloons of my life,
beyond shout and cries of sharp edged knife...

The End Revelation...
The culmination of wondrous sensation.
The all-enveloping radiant shine from above.
The ultimate sublime shrine of 'Great Love'...

Gentle hold of hand and kiss of lip,
wedded flow of conscience fellowship...
The stride and view through flower,
beside your bride in sacred power...

The long beauty song and dance,
lucky chance of beholden calm trance.
The union and communion integration,
knowing forever is for ever – the salvation...

Sensing the single spirit born of two,
romance ballad defined by me and you...
That there is no death of True Love,
those high highs of mind dreamed of...
The flight of morning dove.

That we are for always - till end of days -
to be seen in kind flutter of queen butterfly in spring,

and in sandy azure summer beach shore stays.
To be heard in church bells and choral sing,
and be felt in all life's most tender ways...

Why do you follow me?
White wisp of marshmallow conscience,
exhibit stage of figments imaginary;
options real, or total nonsense.

In a sky of blue, you hang;
a morph parade show of head.
Switch images of claw and fang,
or beauty aspirations instead...

You give look into best soul,
then fade to ugly dark side.
Opening to my heart whole,
or pass me down abyss slide...

You are a wonder of Universe,
connecting current to my insides.
Bringing horror curse, or worse;
or all fine poetic verse provides...

How is it so, that God created a cloud?
To accompany on journey, wherever vowed;
to bring on your wits, or soften scare;
to make caution, or sharpen the dare...

From thin vaporous air, a changing theater -
antagonizing or befriending, invigorating.
Judge and jury of mind, ultimate reasoner -
awaiting my next move to counter, baiting...

Your ever presence above for survival;
revving engine to stay alive, you and I...

A slow churning of our energy revival,
always nearby, never to say goodbye.

From nowhere, she had appeared...
In silence of night, to table she steered...
After bleak long hours in devastating fight,
through the dead and weak – her sight...

A secret commander, they said...
She was brought wine and bread...
Her long dark hair beneath a black beret,
aloft in quiet air; no man with word to say...

Shapely lips and penetrant foggy bottom eyes,
mystery presence and all beauty symbolize...
With all around her in awkward stumbling awe,
awaiting her facial gesture, or swing of claw...

I aware of her total control of hardy men,
a warrior goddess in fighting lions' den...
Known to all, but to me – of spirit free...
Golden tales of bravery, and power energy...

In glow of flickering candle flame, and her halo,
the famed small red rose tattoo on cheek...
On her smooth white skin, it shouted mellow;
but of running blood combat, truth bespeak...

First memory of the girl with black beret,
of my desire to sit and watch, and stay...
To breathe in her airs, and princess flows;
but sensing always her strong martial pose...

How is it still, I know not your name?
An angel such, with so gentle a touch...

With a beauty all your own, fiery flame;
with all the grace and style, as much...

How do you gallop into my life, hurried?
Stay with me awhile, don't wander off.
Tender me your love, leave me unworried.
Dance with me to that land we know, far-off...

How do I not know your name?
With your blazing eyes and spirit,
thunderous sensuous core and game,
what do I call the girl of no limit?

Perhaps, forces of nature need no moniker;
just being is enough, with no more said.
If I were a philosopher, you'd be life's thermometer;
even with all other things left unspoken and unread...

So be kind... Return to me in your swagger.
With your bow and arrow, and golden heart;
with your bandoliers and sharpened dagger;
with voice of singing heaven – never again depart...

In throes of passion in the field...
On the greens, red rose and yellow daffodil;
with all at our sacred yield, in a love sealed;
with the air full of thrill and amorous will...

To feel alive and free, eternally...
Keeping death afar, as the most distant star,
and allowing close only deepest sense be.
Adjoined, you and I, in beauty reservoir...

We have eloped,
away from all ugly sores and scars.
Much further away than we could've ever hoped -

In a canvas of mind, of the best Renoirs...

In our ideal, hand in hand -
with lips and hearts fused
on glorious promised land,
never our love refused...

Could this be you?
This air that comes to me,
from expanse of all star I see?
Can it be thee?

This soft wind song treble,
from cosmic gas and dust formation;
a settled tremble from highest level,
of far off light pillars of creation.

The tender warm blow,
from distant exploding suns;
giver of iron for blood marrow,
and oxygen for lungs...

Let it once calm and soothe,
then harden the calcium in bone.
Leave my tattered edges smooth,
but too carry my spear at enemy known...

In my rumbling imaginings,
actions of a levitated mind;
in the tight soul fastenings,
and all memory left behind...

This air that envelops me,
that flows from toe to head;
from glory sky and sea that be,
and prepares for all things ahead...

The ocean between us...
I, counting days on solar abacus;
envisioning a meeting that may not come,
listening to slow beat of martial drum.

I would fly to you, if I had wings.
I would fight all kings,
and take on all that brings -
armed only with rocks and slings...

For there is no life for me without you,
no space on earth without thee true;
like bow without arrow,
or sight of open sea without narrow,
or no blood in the marrow...

So, I will seek forevermore;
sail the seven seas of lore,
until there is nothing of me for.
Fight each battle of every war...

I will never cease to see,
your angel face with me -
your velvet lips and jewel eyes,
heart and soul of all I fantasize...

For there can be only one love...
One energy from above.
If I cannot have thee,
I no longer want to be...

In my driving tempest of thought:
Intense moving pictures in brain,
of great wishes and dreams sought,

of high golden ring ideals to gain...

To be made of warrior steel –
but with kind heart of honey;
fast to feel, yet quicker to heal,
in unstoppable holy journey...

On the only path to take:
The solo real, not the fake -
of love and honor,
and none other...

Never fooled by false appeal,
bag of money or heavy meal.
Moving only to front with destiny seal;
shoot for far-off star surreal...

Rare fair air of virtue trail,
of pink horse and purple whale.
Track of sugar candy and eternal youth,
soft love melody and tender heart soothe...

To come out of body cast -
leave the earthly to heavenly,
in army of Universe vast.
Reach for you so desperately,
breathlessly...

In a secret split cosmic second –
Destiny of Universe was decreed;
fate of Earth and Man was too indeed.
In our twin heart was born hopeful seed.

From none to all, in explosive burst,
elemental cloud of stardust dispersed.
From less than zero, to infinite count -

nothing nowhere, to all things paramount.

Grow star nursery, to system and galaxy,
ever expansion with no conceivable finality.
Endless Space, from where to where -
no lines or borders, start to finish despair.

In small time fraction of second datum -
less measure than a God finger snap,
was born building block chemical atom
and Creation's budding celestial map...

Later on Earth, in prophetic speed,
the wind and unwind of double helix;
in mud pots and water stream need,
the mysteries of life's reproduction fix...

The living from unliving substrate,
DNA's opportunity to cast beating color.
To narrate cell breath from empty slate,
taking directive from All-Mighty Caller...

From random mutations in Evolution,
hair split moments decide genetic fate.
Rise of Man from nucleotide substitution,
great magic trait in a Time instant rate...

So, what of you and I;
of wondrous microsecond, eye to eye;
the first gaze and heart stop moment;
passion thought and songful poetic romaunt?

In so little time, the ligature bind...
To be no longer part, but the whole;
love blind in a world so disinclined.
So, what of the heart and soul?

In such tiny a meter, a period so fleet;
in such quick incomprehensible feat -
the plans for a Universe can glow unfurl;
and from gas and dust swirl – an Earth pearl...

In fast pace, so too can arrive:
the tender kiss and hand of *amor* alive.
In rapid immediate and wink of an eye:
the end of soul search of red string tie...

So, in our contemplation of cosmic split second;
of all fine creative beauty born of spontaneity;
of all suns and moons and spinning globes, I reckon;
of all love holds and flaming fire instant electricity...

In that same cosmic split-second measure:
Man can wipe away all brilliant ingenuity;
end our imaginative Earth, for all of us – no more
treasure;
vanish off all trails of hearts – lost loves in perpetuity...

In vacuum silence, in isolation...
All things motionless, but my heart;
Time dilation, in endless flotation;
lost, suspended in no end or start...

In a dark, dark, black world I be:
in closed globe of sightless sea and sky.
Without a vision or a sound, but thee:
in beat of core muscle refusing to die.

The cadence of Mind Love...
The regular rhythm flow of blood.
The elation and sorrows, poets write of.
The rush of imagery and passion flood...

I want to live!
To perish into nothing – No!
From less than zero, to outpour give;
push on, my heart – don't let go...

I ask only for a chance, a breakthrough -
To leave this abyss void infinitude,
and fly like invincible eagle to you.
To have again your love, in sanctitude...

For in the end of all end,
at finish of one-way road true,
on Time's path in her final bend,
there can be only Veritas – and You...

In my misty sight... Land!
And a beach of white sand...
Mountains tall, and sky of blue.
Oh, what a view!

In faith, it is my destination.
God has heard my oration.
Now give me strength to fight;
put power in bones, and eyes alight.

I will pray for my girl with black beret,
red rose on cheek and feet of ballet.
May she be here, waiting -
safe from fear, with heart pulsating...

I have arrived, at last -
to protect, and reach for the past.
My cells will multiply in task...
We will embrace in glow of glory bask.

Our sphere - a tiny spinning dot in a vast infinite,
sailing through a forever endless dark blue.
A spot overlook in magnificent nature innocent;
from true where or when, I have not a clue…

Our sphere, graced by mighty creative minds -
to conjure and perform historic good of all kinds,
to reveal moving music sounds that soothe,
and color pictures and vital books of Truth…

Our sphere – with secret code of life in hand,
with chemistry structure of memory DNA and cell,
with more and more deep science secrets grand,
and all harvest of quantum atom as well…

Our sphere – in the four dimensions of Space-Time,
in the magic dance of swirling gas ether clouds,
in elated ballad poetry of 'Great Creator Prime' - -
has also seen dark poison of dictator shrouds…

In all this fine and pure, so much evil bad:
examples of Warsaw, and Dresden, and Stalingrad…
The romps of crazy kings and despot rules,
religious false crusades and massacres of fools…

I wish to sleep now…
May neurons slow altered state of matter -
the fire and re-fire, to peace slumber allow.
No killing, only love – and only envelopment of latter…

From where have I come to this island of dream?
From what bloody soil have I been delivered?
What have my eyes seen in bloodstream scream?
And reasons for body and heart and soul shivered?

Mighty World

In this world,
in this mighty world -
on Earth of cold natural selection
and furious biological rejection;
globe of trophy survival of fittest
and death burial of all but quickest;
Time and Space of Newton and Galileo,
quantum mechanics and orbital paseo;
microcosm of animal cell and nucleus,
secretive nucleic acids of Olympus...

Who are we?
Where do we come from?
Where are we going?
Why and when?

In this world,
in this mighty world -
in lands of empty churches and temples,
social crumbles and decrepit symbols;
forgotten beauty sonnets of Shakespeare,
Verdi and Puccini romance songs disappear;
of hard deaf ears to Bach and Beethoven,
and no longer Plato and Aristotle plainspoken;
long lost words of Homer and Tolstoy,
discarded lessons of Helen and Troy...

Who are we?
Where do we come from?
Where are we going?
Why and when?

In this world,

in this mighty world -
in halls of forsaken strokes of Guernica and Sistine,
nostalgia of lost colors of Kandinsky and Dali pristine;
in hurt of missing sensuous forms of Claudel and Rodin,
and unattended ancient sculptures of creation
caveman;
unnoticed bleeding feather edges of Rothko blocks,
and invisible trauma streaks of Richter and Kiefer shocks;
hidden but learned brush sweeps of sensitive Basquiat;
all gone, unperceived, no traces in total evaporate –
Now only my spirit as mascot...

Search for Immortality

Man's never ceasing search for immortality -
striving creative souls on fire gone mad.
The rise and fight of true hero odyssey -
no conform to culture, barren desert nomad.

Flight from sickle, denial of death;
join group of common, escape forget;
placation, follow rules for breath - -
or seek eternal achieve, live out - yet...

Simple Man, too lazy to see cold reality;
easy wash of brain and follow orders out.
Avoid shadow and sleep well in felicity,
run from hounds of hell toothy snout.

Group with religion and creed above all,
frame battle against foreign in forever wars.
Gather from plural, in false amaranth hall;
fool oneself as member of 'never-dying' corps.

Finer to release pretense dogma and vice;
travel above beyond, throw high spirit dice;
transcend through science and art portal;
attain the untouchable, live the unforgettable,
heal the incurable, solve the impossible;
be forever immortal...

Passage of Time

Giant wrinkles in unknown far Space,
in white dress satin and soft pink lace;
measured in fond memory recall base,
deep weathered lines of fine furrow face.

What is Time to Man and his general clan?
Big sensations and dream cortex imaginations?
Alas! The ticking human watch complications,
and emotion-touched wild heart palpitations...

I remember you in hidden reconcile:
blazing eyes and tender smile,
the elegant style profile,
cosmic sundial - stunned immobile...
Your delicate body forms,
and erotic swarms –
stopping storm and rain,
and all universe Time profane...

To grasp and impede atomic clock,
slow the angel sounds of Bach.
Love me, and pass on your voltage shock...

The still, before impact moment explosion.
The resonance hum grows in slow motion,
outpouring the valentine devotion...

Go on forever!
Deter the detested life meter!
Never cease, Eternal Queen –
silk and passion work machine!
Forget things sensed between!
Never mind Einstein sublime,
halt the dooming passage of Time...

Eyes of Defiance

Our eyes of defiance...
The true blues of bruise...
No alliance – war of noncompliance...
Forget lying views, reject excuse...

No more tall tales, avoid tear trails;
listen to inner good demon,
break away from hard fails;
rid the chains, be a freeman.

Don't take flight,
stand and fight.
No wrong, just right;
out of shadow, to the light.

Hold strong the courage;
don't thwart, encourage.
Stride with pride,
turn back evil tide.

Speed the heart,
ready martial art.
No retreat, no surrender;
no pretender, only defender.

Defiance - - -
Our last and best tool
of fine moral reliance.
No more cruel, no ridicule;
no longer eyes of the fool...

Tremble of the Night

In tremble of the night - - -
Low light, heading for a gunfight.
Men and women along the line,
long shadows under moonshine.

Trenches three-deep full of spirit;
doom and scent of death, near it...
Silent air, full of doubt and brave fear;
but no screams or wails, not a tear...

For love of God and country, for humanity.
To rid us of further strife and agony.
No more loss, only combat for victory.
War of nation, human heart tragedy.

Gaze on each other, bond and trust.
All unknown future, most into dust.
Soft nod of head and wink of sure eye,
knowing certain some of us will die.

Then the rumble - deep shake of earth,
across distant ground in pitch darkness.
Clamor of iron - enemy unnatural birth,
Red tanks to tread over our carcass.

Under light of star, you are next to me...
The lash of orbs and face of beauty...
Courageous girl, love of my life be...
Under attack, but still our sight free...

Your fine long hair under wool beret,

moon glow on glory cheeks and lips.
In this one moment, I wish ever stay;
soul union, tender touch of fingertips.

To brace you in my arms, love you...
To hold on forever and ever more...
At least until sun and morning dew,
or hand in hand thru eternity door.

Mouth on warm lovely mouth gentle,
transfer inner spirit into each other...
Love elemental, passion monumental -
slip this life together, to find another...

Flash guns now come, thunder light...
Last embrace, last loving hopeful kiss...
Futures away, in tremble of the night...
Always, devotion never amiss...

We Were Children, Once

In the thick warm tropical haze
and memory of lost bygone days,
thru flutter of wind past limb of tree,
it all - at once - comes flowing into me...

We were children, once – long ago;
when times were golden without woe.
Sleep was kind and complete – full night;
and morning was born in all its glory light.

We played, and lay on greenest grass;
and ran faraway under clearest sky.
We shared with truest friends in class;
and always sure thought, we'd never die...

In moon and star dream life, we belonged;
in time prolonged, we felt never wronged.
To live a million years in fresh young minds -
to cherish, and relish in love that binds...

So, what became of friends in story zest;
the bonds of spirit care held the best?
Of alliance, and sense of eternal assurance?
At least, it can be said in absence - - -
We were children, once...

Dystopia

Don't you appreciate, understand, see?
They desire only strong worker bee -
Not in communal pair synergy, but three;
one push, another pull, and central referee...

To keep humanity always labor busy,
regardless of effectual productivity;
to dumb down brain and drain insane,
muscle-bots in long gang factory chain.

Moving mountains and digging ditches,
running machines with nervous twitches.
Making nothing more than useless things,
pound the body picadillo until it stings.

Off with bell, to home and play -
video game box, remote display.
Push buttons on electronic tray;
donkey replay away, rest of day.

No true knowledge or wisdom,
no self-awareness or optimism,
no religious worship or patriotism,
only terror victim of Red socialism.

Without sex inclination, without gender;
without sing of song or poem splendor.
No dance or love romance weekender,
only blank soul and void spirit surrender.

To bed, and six hours of monitored sleep;
no fancy dreams allowed, or toilet break.

Magic ray to sap memory of cretin sheep.
Neuter nature with anti-rebel iv drug shake.

The amblyopia of a near future dystopia ---
a complete hellhole coming apocalypse,
a heartless bleak wasteland cornucopia,
a human civilization total eclipse...

A Walk Through Trees

A morning walk through cool shade of trees.
Autumn forest dark, of red, green, and brown.
Encampment along blue stream to crash and seize;
must now attack – not break, fall, or back down...

Men and women, many hundreds across,
move silent through dry leaf and brush.
Cover ground of golden lichen and moss,
creep by little step - prepare for final rush.

Downhill, we now run with pointed bayonets;
slash and stab, and kill as all anger besets.
At anything that stands and breathes, we shoot;
with no salute, we decide the savage dispute.

At end, I sit at stream and wash away guilt.
Red blood murder ebbs from me down water.
Crimson scarlet mixing with aqua blue silt;
river and skin gone clean, lives to higher altar...

To regroup and mend, no condolences to send;
with another battle fought, more minds to tend.
From fury to sorrow, in heart and marrow -
No judge or jury, no soul to lend or borrow.

So, what is this sick and empty wicked feel?
The lives we steal, with such civil war zeal...
To what high holy ideal, do we appeal?
Or is it not our own demise in this ordeal,
that we reveal and seal?
Our Achilles heel...

Animalization of Man

In the dehumanization of 'Wise Man';
in removal of 'sapiens sapiens' from Homo;
in making modern group culture, joining clan;
conforming brain, to bug segmented entomo-

From our own subconscious denial of death,
need to 'fit right' into the similar and familiar.
Create xenophobic hate for 'unlikes' in same breath,
whisper evil of those 'non-people' we deem inferior.

The psychic inability to accept own certain demise;
threat sense of being overrun, wiped out, going to zero;
internal fear of being 'unimportant' in cosmic comprise;
we make ourselves 'bigger', concoct phantom culture
hero.

A psychological trick of the mind – a strange hocus
pocus;
self-inflicted misunderstanding, rejection of
'incompatibles';
unleash pain and harm in dehumanized defocus
atrocious;
genocide 'people who are not people', slaughterhouse
animals.

Is this the only destiny of past, present, and future Man?
To blood spill and kill, against all reason and good will?
To follow the vile demagogic, and psycho-pathologic?
Rage and raze and mass destroy, and crematorium fill?

Are neurotransmitters of the brain, a biological illogical?

Would it not be better to redirect action potential;
harness the wild beast, tender the mind gentle?
Be prudential, get to the core of heart essential;
raise spirit transcendental to just kind monumental?

Would it be asking too much for Man to think?
Is 'Homo sapiens sapiens' a misnomer?
Is it possible to tame a rabid fox, on the brink?
Can we be sober, and grow to utopia beholder?

I do not know answers to these difficult questions,
but I will do my best to lessen the tensions.
I will make my own confessions, and take lessons;
consider connections, and forgive transgressions.
I will seek to leave only finest human impressions…

Act II

Land

In the global annihilation of total 'End War', cities and nations of the world are erased. The culture of 'civilized' Man is wiped from cosmic history. Shortly following the missiles, the ensuing nuclear climate continues to kill all life forms. The Earth returns to an unlivable primitive state.

Yet, it is in the 'After War' - where sapient soul spirit of Homo sapiens sapiens is lost. It is in this stage of the dissolution of Modern Man, where DNA makes its truest presence known...

I had seen the 'Four Horsemen'...
Pestilence and famine,
much war and death,
beat our nation path...

The six ages of lost empire –
pioneer discovery and conquest fire;
power commerce, and all affluent surplus;
bearing intellect, to bread and circus;
... decadence...

Fake fiat float and bipolar market,
corporatization of freedom ticket.
Financial pandemic, no security blanket.
False geo-politik and military picket.

Total war waged across enraged globe –
nuke and chemical weapons, and killer microbe.
Scorched earth and sky, and fallen cities,
after broken brains and forgotten treaties.

With loss of nations, no law and order;
survivor mob hordes in chaos horror.
In time - formation of gladiator armies,
and fight for few resource necessities.

I, a teacher of literature and mathematics,
am now captain of Blue freedom battalion.
I learned the ways of combat systematics,
and have become a leader dragon assassin.

Through field glass, I surveyed the battleground.
Across murder soil, bloodied red in white morning fog,
in tree line spotted – dark feathered owl with yellow eyes
round.
With one shot, I ended his unwanted menace look
monologue.

Like I, hooty owl had seen the evil barbarism display:
plain of close quarter knife and gun, predator and prey.
He seemed to say of D-Day, in many more than one
way,
that sinister vile of human decay was here to ever stay.

I could not overcome, as I peered into his wise eyes,
the bad reflections of my innermost lost soul inside.
He knew, as I, the evil done – the cause of hateful cries.

The owl became unpleasant guide to all wicked
applied.

So, I took his life, as I had taken all the others.
Deserving or undeserving, it did not matter to me.
Those I'd killed were enemy, not sisters or brothers.
With guarantee, I would not allow even one to flee.

Alas, poor bird went down like foe to ground.
His blood mixed into earth with all other 'animals',
to help nourish soils for next crops profound.
No remorse whatsoever for enemy cannibals.

And why should I care, with all there was to bear?
Our people, torn and frayed, in hungry despair;
with so little field, unpoisoned by venomous air;
and rare water to drink, untouched by inhumane affair.

Yes... Naturally, the apocalypse had brought civil war.
Basic instincts had formed killers of peaceful civilians.
Human intelligence for survival had made leaders roar,
and followers galore... perhaps, in the angry millions...

I grabbed my pistol and walked the plain.
Lift of fog and harsh sun stenched drain of slain.
I ordered men to fan out and place final bullets;
show a little grace we had remaining, to fullest.

We had caught these Red soldiers by surprise.
In the black night, machine guns ripped them away.
With ease in dirty hell, they fell in quick demise.
Unlucky few, who had not, were pounced in disarray.

As in many times past, our spy – U – had saved the day.
Intelligence source behind Red lines had forewarned.
Identity unknown to all, even our tall leaders without say,
U messages would prepare us for attacks scorned.

Shot of my pistol into heads of those few still breathing.
Then, silence after combat, not a voice to be heard.
We'd leave them bleeding for hours, the soil needing.
Defeated bodies fertilizing, even the knowing bird.

How evil we can be, even I – raised in romantic English
poetry;
educated with music and number and knowledge of the
stars.
Comfortable in my skin, I'd been; aware of verse
symmetry.
How wrong I was – I knew; I had once preferred Venus
over Mars.

I fast paced to nearby blue sea.
I threw myself into the surf, to cleanse.
Leaving my men to forage ground without me,
I looked back through mind's eye lens...

They picked clean the Red bastards.
Any useful thing was taken with delight.
Techniques of search had been mastered;
pockets with seed or jewel emptied in spite.

We, lawless renegades, caught in a vise.
To live, we needed to kill and steal precise.
We were extreme professional murderers and thieves;
cut-throat artists of pain, and all that darkness weaves.

But how? I asked. How had the world come to this?
Of same brain domain of true greatness attain,
to barbarity submiss of deep and dark abyss.
From semi-ordered planet, to entropy insane...

And I myself? I asked...

An old believer of good and true.
A beholder of all beauty of the past.
A seer of the long love view.

How had I come to this unholy place,
to this plateau of ever more disgrace?
Had my genome mutated in debase,
and human race gone to null space?

Beyond crested waves, to other side;
over angry ocean, aqua teal and wide;
rose the 'Island' from disturbed floor of Earth,
after violent bomb detonations of warring birth.

Tales of peaceful shores and calm green hills,
and passes from sea through color flower fields;
of white sands and lush verdant forest fulfills,
and far plains of beauty and plenty crop yields...

It had been long said, by those who surely knew,
and secret messages passed on by agents of U -
that dreamy 'Isle of Life' held cool spring fountains
and rushing creeks flowing from tranquil mountains.

I wished one day to see special outcropping ideal;
perhaps, it could be a settled place of gentle liberty.
An isolate for personal freedom, a place to rest and
heal,
offering escape from miserable hostility –
A search for Trinity...

My old land, my locale of nativity and delivery,
where I had grown to man in joyous harmony,
was now an infernal burning hole of ugly destiny,
and center stage for crazy Man's unholy cruelty.

If stories were true, of island with such serene world view -
I'd swim myself alone across sea, to that lost Eden be,
and plant future family onto soils free under sky blue,
with airs to fill ears and hearts with songs of sweet
melody.

But for now, it was only an oneiric fantasy...
I, a captain of fighting battalion, had great chore –
to protect and serve discarded people in sacred duty,
and offer encore after Great War –
act as final guarantor.

My present role and task, for any out there who may ask,
was only to defend simple human flock from evil pagan
stock;
to hold oppressive Red surge with their evil devil death
mask,
and provide final hinder to sad 'After War' unjust shock.

Thus, now back to killing and thievery – loss of mind and
body...
We, to escape own demise, had become monstrous
epitome
of the very horrors and hideous traits we battled so
diligently.
From inside our own very hearts had grown cancer
indignity...

We blamed hateful Reds and their lack of Holy Spirit...
Yet, I understood my job was as much to secure
my faithful people's true soul as it was to steer it.
What good was victory for liberty, without moral cure?

Could a free people last even a single day,
knowing deep inside themselves real truth
of abusive vengeance and retribution stray?

To live on after sinful deed and lying untruth?

In all vicious ungodly awful done on us,
in massacres and burnings of entire villages;
in rapes and murders of innocents, abnormous;
in all blood spillages and genocide terror images...

I must remember and remind order of day and night,
bang of heavy sword on shield and roll of fast drum,
call of justice and Holy Spirit in heat of battle fight –
recall pursue sum of honor virtue, from where we come...

In evening, at village tavern,
at table with gas light lantern;
surrounded by men and women of war,
with story of battle, and more...

Thrown down shots of whiskey and wine,
a genuine strengthening of war spine.
Sounds of harmonica and song,
long the hours – and strong...

Sense forbode, of future erode,
feeling of living on time borrowed.
With numb of alcohol flow in vein,
slow mellow drain of worried brain...

Talk of freedom and good life past,
and pallid denuded world today in contrast.
Discuss and argue of where hope had gone,
and even whether we'd see another rise of dawn.

In loud commotion of music and word,
in ruckus din of flail and thrust of fist,
walked in young woman of beauty absurd,
leaving all present – in lofty midst.

Tall girl of shapely form,
with sentient eyes and shock lips;
with firestorm glare, but face warm,
and general stun of star apocalypse.

Girl with bandoliers and black beret,
with dark hair and look of thunder.
Her motion ballet to cast ships away,
traits of wonder to bury our world under.

I heard man say, she was brigade commander,
from the high north in southern retreat.
A Blue guerrilla fighter, highlander of no surrender,
was now running from Red overheat.

Tyrant onslaught against us was driving down,
cornering in lower peninsula, in last village Blue town.
We now had no exits around, only fall into the sea.
Like hopeless at Dunkirk, death defeat of ultimate
degree.

I moved toward her, to the bar line.
Aside, our eyes and minds met in melt divine.
With hand on carbine, she sipped her wine,
but steady went her other hand into mine...

'Hello...' I said tender, with gentle touch.
In great clamor, a silence awe such.
A smile greeting from her, an invitation:
flirtation for Time cessation and Love creation.

In unexplained of purely unexplainable,
in tight suffocate stress of last hoorah,
we joined hearts in bond unbreakable,
and held each other under golden aura...

She said to me, 'I am here for thee,
'to fill your spirit in final graceful plea.'
As if we had been forever, I understood:
the breadth and depth of the very good...

In girl with black beret, in her run to the south,
I saw all that had escaped me – in past and present.
As if treasured aisle had opened to our heaven's mouth,
and hand in hand, off we went in a grand ascent...

Next morning, before light of misty daybreak,
in quiet darkness, along high rocky ridge line,
after embrace and perhaps last handshake,
we descended slope – thru green palm and pine.

We hundreds, we last unlucky fortunate few,
taking combat charge with secret intel from U –
passed in silence to enemy camp by stream,
with bayonet and sword, and all sharp extreme.

Without sound, we came to fight and retake –
the only river escape to free ocean outbreak.
We were intent to hold to last standing man,
and allow free flight of each child and woman.

With cold wind toss, thru branch of tree,
I looked across long dark Blue row for thee.
A low musical whistling tone with air blown,
cries of family and many friends lost bemoan...

Of girl with black beret, what more could I say?
How could spirits entangle in such Planck Time -
in a trillionth of second, in that split of day,
in a short sweet chime of long universe climb?

In small remaining night, I could not see her.

Her form and way, missed in the dark display.
With all that could occur, I desired in giant blur.
I wanted – I needed – to glimpse before the fray.

Finally, at last, I caught nature's pink of lips;
under sliver of remainder moon, I felt the swoon.
Too far to kiss, too far to touch with fingertips,
I looked away and drove down to Red commune.

Ankle deep sprint thru water splash,
fire run frenzy, flesh cut and slash.
Steel to cold steel frontal assault clash,
stab straight thru and rapid gun flash.

Yells and screams, battle of opposite teams;
no mercy shown in land of idea regimes.
Surprise attack, recon Reds are beaten -
all, they fall, in state of confusion weaken.

Madness of an hour, violent anger empower;
stamp out of sick weed and old nation flower.
Onto the ground, they go; to bleed their seed
into soil, we plead, of our future unborn freed.

In early light, in brilliance of sun reward -
I steer toward large stone on edge of watery brook,
and rest remains of dawn and victory scored.
I peer down into the sea from rocky overlook.

Distant invisible horizon of my people and country,
I gaze into unknown future fates and toils;
real or surreal – in truth of mind elementary –
unholy and detestable, whatever war's spoils.

Where was this 'Island' they spoke of,
this hidden peaceful Garden of Eden?
Holding healing springs and white dove,

where true love can flourish and deepen.

I stare into thin and straight blue line,
between airy Heaven and the dense Earth,
separating sea and sky – the deep and shine.
I could not see this isle, this fortress of rebirth.

During dream of odd ethereal sight,
lost and disabled in morning light -
with drip of my blood, and of those I'd taken,
into rushing stream and world forsaken.

The beating heart – muscle of emotion –
lashing out at all around me in commotion.
With each full fill and strong force contraction,
a painful eating out of my life in subtraction.

So, to where from here?
Where do I march, after the cleanse?
After evacuate of innocent lady and child so dear,
do I fight on forever, and deal with all contends?

Girl with black beret passed me her hand.
Under radiant light, where nothing can hide;
with all ugly blemish and beauty glory strand,
from waste to dreamland, my soul now fortified.

We walked together into flower fields,
beyond river and deep forest stands,
with laid down weapons and war shields,
into green pastures and color homelands.

We lay on glisten dew of bright and bold day,
and melted our love into hearth of earth.
In mighty struggle for life and death delay,
we wished only to give our total energy worth...

'And your name, Girl?
'Your call from childhood?'
I kissed her, and touched below beret a hair curl.
I gazed into eyes of womanhood.

She said, 'In our troubles,
'in our times of freedom struggles,
'no need for names of flames,
'just the joy heart exclaims.'

She held my hand, and on her toes,
and with bosom against my chest,
and soft white cheek of gentle rose -
the girl kissed my lips in holy blessed.

'In contact of heart to heart,
'where flows of mind and soul go,
'no spoken call to name impart,
'only show emotive of love aglow.

'No time to sense burden of place,
'no thought of past or future trace,
'only the now, and our present space,
'remember our saving grace –
'just in case.'

The girl spoke with angel voice,
deep wisdom of old soul spirit.
She praised white silk rejoice,
and red lace hot passion minute.

A sudden moment of her love bestowment,
in instant know of our tender desire throe,
in our hidden guilts and needs for atonement -
we allowed for pleasure in Time forego...

So, in flower field, on rare verdant plateau,
in world of dark shadow and ugly outgrow,
under seldom seen, blue and green - rainbow,
we passed the time allegro, even so...

For in love from nowhere, in nowhere -
when soon, as set of sun and rise of moon,
girl with black beret would run the stream to 'Isle',
and so too our dream, and all things worthwhile.

In my days of boy and man, and recent war span,
I'd sensed much loss and young life expire.
I'd worked my way thru feeling, tho less than,
I'd hoped in our ever dismal global hellfire...

Never able to accommodate farewell:
good day – good night – so long – and just get by.
Memory sear, as well, in long constant retell;
but with this girl, this one fine girl – in all hurtful cry –
there could never ever be final embrace goodbye...

Many days passed before great night battle.
With women and children gone to river,
to ocean, and distant bastion of isle Babel -
all hoped for survival and peace deliver.

Stage set for final strong defense.
Along shore upstream, combat teams
aligned in trenches before intense commence;
prepared to stop the Reds by any means.

The girl commander, the non-bystander,
had refused to escape away safely.
She stood next to me like Athena, but grander,
holding long gun and bayonet, bravely.

In evening cold, under wide moon bold,
one could hear songs and stories told.
Many pats on the back, and smiles no lack,
waiting for attack in frigid night black.

Words said before upheaval,
between brothers in arms facing evil.
Nods of the head, and winks of eye,
given friendly before angst of war cry.

Into eyes of girl with black beret,
I peered... Steady and long, I revered.
Falling slow into depths of soul convey,
I softly steered - and disappeared.

Like sudden great fall into a wishing well,
when hope turns to dread of death knell,
I caught myself desiring all of the universe -
but fearing end adverse, and even worse.

In strange mix of beauty and pain,
with all the world to lose, and all to gain,
I fell... into eternal space without bottom,
without underside, deep and solemn...

The girl saw my unsteady balance,
 and kindly quick stiffened my spine...
She kissed me, long and hard into valiance,
and returned me to hero blood line...

Our last embrace, in light of sky flares
and booming guns, in grind of steel,
and foul smoky air's violent tears --
Our hearts in a thump to thump final appeal...

After long win of the night and next day,
with only we – the victors – left alive to say;
after clearing of our dead from the ground,
and carrying off of the few wound-bound...

We retrenched ourselves along Blue line,
and waited for next Red counter-attack.
With strong urge, battle girl with lips of wine
had ferried the hurt down river to sea track.

I stayed behind, along the gutter, to fight.
In our cause, so bleak dim with no light,
we hoped to give time for others' escape -
and possibly cause a short war re-shape.

The girl with black beret – with no name –
reluctant to leave me and the cause,
had floated away toward isle of magic fame,
to guide the injured and maim in the pause.

I and my final hundred would either win,
or lose last piece of freedom turf...
Our empire, our old 'liberty has been',
had been wiped from map into the surf.

With poor leadership and loss of morale,
in crazy global wars and bizarre genocides,
our once great nation fell into a grand mal.
Bewildered survivors had not healed divides.

Thus began – End of Days – of sweet Motherland;
and with it, end of me and mine in land I loved.
Where I had led my life as courage heart planned,
and learned ways of manhood roved and carved.

I peered through gun scope across trodden soil:

large open field bloodied and beaten to earthy pulp,
tall forest canopy poisoned by toxic air spoil,
falling rocket and mortar into deep crater sculp.

Dead stumpy trees, no leaves, and ground without grass
- -
Old green and blue breathing world dead at our hands.
Life sacred pummeled into rotten stinking mass;
even insects could not survive these vile badlands.

Through scope, I viewed Red commie moving thru low
brush.
I sighted careful, and fired one sneaky round into his
head.
Brains splattered over hidden comrades, now in mad
rush.
I deep inspired and held, shooting trigger and creating
more dead.

All Reds were bad, and so too were many Blues...
In the 'After War', the good were extinct; we were all to
lose.
Primal instincts, born of Darwin genome, had taken over.
The need to kill every last Red I saw, with not one
leftover.

I fired and fired until finger numb at close of day.
Still no counter-attack. Cold night returned without
moon.
Along trenches, my men waited for enemy to show way -
we outnumbered, and sure to lose our wits and lives
soon.

More flares lit the sky red pink;
then the screams, 'Gas!' into the brink.
Only a few of the Blue had masks,

the others stiffened to fulfill tasks.

I gave my chemical protector to a boy,
not older than fourteen, in the obscene.
Next came artillery in final assault ploy,
before the armor and infantry in screen.

Without mask, many died in the mustard.
The rest readied fire toward Red bastard.
Came the tanks, invisible grind in the smoked;
I nearly blind and in choke, all fears evoked.

In short reprieve, in the mind sieve,
in flying bullet and bomb through air -
image of thee, and all splendor to relive,
comes fast to me in all your beauty fair.

Beneath tough *guerillera* thin,
under coat of rough armor chain -
lay all gentle senses of Venus within,
and the wonders of paradise reign.

In deadly fire I face, I stand and brace,
and hope to see again my girl of placid grace.
I will survive to breathe anew the sultry scent
of girl from heaven and gods of love invent.

Thousands of Red demons from no-man's land
surged at final trench of freedom in homeland.
In black devil gear, and sticking steel bayonets,
they poured into us like hell's molten assets.

The final fall of liberty and all remains of sensibility,
the erasure of democratic nobility and humility...
Epochs earned of human progress in science,
the arts, and statesmanship of grand alliance...

To have turned cosmic clock of the world to nothing,
and not gained even something...
For all the stubborn religions to have passed
fast thru the ages, and not scored at last...

To have destroyed all good creations of the mind,
collected in libraries since beginning of Time...
To leave us all culturally starved and blind,
without even a trace of faith sublime...

Leaders of the world had done all this.
Kiss and moral bliss thrown into the abyss.
Four billion years of rare Earth tossed away,
like garbage evil betray into final doomsday.

Hot bullet sheared off complete my left ear,
and left me ringing numb in total silence.
Another to shoulder blew me asleep to rear,
and onto wood raft on river without guidance.

You are quiet eye of cyclone,
soft dream in the nightmare.
In mind tempest, I am not alone;
in the mad incubus, you are there...

Set me adrift on course, free to you;
guiding star in hazed obscure view.
From spiral squall, pass me to center;
to glory hall, and allow me to enter...

In fires, I've been.
On mountains, I've climbed.
The glory, and sin;
breaks of souls, loves that bind.

In heart of mine...
In seams of Time, long line...
In deep salvation search...
From depths of hell, or heaven perch...

The arduous road to Truth,
 with its bends and forks;
to old age from youth,
with silks and angry torques.

At end, a final reveal -
that in spinning wheel of life,
in final embrace and kiss ideal -
only you, and you – my wife...

Impermanence of Permanence

The short or long day is measured from rising sun;
seconds, minutes, and hours in the imaginative mind.
Calendar clicks when lights are gone and done,
repeating cold symbols of clock Time well defined.

Months and years pass lines of punish gauntlet;
cherished tears counted off slow in rhythm sequence.
Loves and fears in numbered droplet from golden
goblet--
All blind trust and follow in math and reason credence.

Is there any permanence in fast run of a charged life?
Do all things, material and mental, wither and dissolve?
Does tick and tock wash away world beauty rife?
Do bad musings of Man, sins and wrongs, also absolve?

In troubled inconstancy of seeming constancy,
in tired inconsistency of ostensible consistency,
even in our angel world of kissing heart and glory hand -
Where do you and I, dearest and purest Love, stand?

When yet tall mountain rows crumble to dust,
and 'endless' noble radiant light drench of sun ends;
when flurries of high sky winds die and no longer gust,
and all spring bird and tree and flower – all life descends.

In a startling universe of ever permanent impermanence,
where eternal energies forever flow in counter direction;

where constant physical change only increases
turbulence,
and heaven bodies reconfigure in atomic resurrection.

What happens, then, to beat of heart on heart - -
our crush lock embrace in eyes and lips and tongues?
Share of song and wine, the beauty of sensual art - -
primitive screams and love shouts from the lungs?

And the love caress and tender whispers in ear?
Passage of warm soothing hands across the rear?
And press of finger flesh to wipe away a trailing tear?
The words of our love, the soft gentle breaths I hear?

In my adoration, in my dearest sincerest thoughts of you;
your wondrous spirit entwined with mine in rich passion
hue;
our bonded souls alive and free in plea, *amor* thru and
thru;
our ghosts refusing impermanence, of the love
permanence,
we knew...

You

Like volatile Mercury - -
I stand at edge of flat Earth.
My body beaten, liquid skin and bones;
long rough road taken from distant birth.
Many hard stones, and pained sorrow groans...

From early strong flesh, to soft and bruised -
hair lost, waxy eyes sunken and crossed.
Past fast mind - weak; at times, even confused.
God knows, I've paid a heavy cost...

Deep run lines and furrows on face,
each cave and crevice with story to tell - -
Many a space of harmony and kind grace,
and too many of sad spirit as well.

In far away ocean blue of iris too,
passages of time come flying thru;
of people I knew, and of things I'd do;
but mostly, of moments spent with you...

In fugue, I am – between here and there;
a dream state, an altered wait at the gate.
I stare in light air - wishing to again share,
reaching with all might for love soul mate.

From tenuous perch, I see a sky of stars:
every Heaven body, also Venus and Mars.
Shining white, haloes of all red and green hue - -
In dark blue, every twinkle ever light of you.

Alone I've been, but not for long more...

In constant gentle memory of day we met.
Your look, the soar of your inner heart core - -
Tender tight bindings of your amorous net.

To live on forevermore in love youth,
with passion songs and poems of joy;
with no stronger rage or musical truth,
than hot fusion and blend of girl and boy.

Oh!
Please Woman, allow me to pursue – for all I need is you.
Grant a final sacred wish, for this old bag of used sinew:
To plunge like lightning bolt from precipice earth untrue,
and grasp and hold dear only hope and faith I ever
knew - -
YOU...

The Struggle

Why does Man covet control over other Men?
Whether bad intent rich, or good poor cheap;
with sword and gun, or flute and fountain pen;
in living color life, or infernal eternal black sleep...

A walk across the bio-science campus:
Research experiments with laws of nature - -
Workers never fear to start over canvas,
if end results don't nurture answer feature.

Devoted scientists mix and match old and new ideas,
titrating thoughts of chemical mass and volume;
never asking what 'is' is, only what science truth degree
is.
Watchful eyes of giant hero figures past - always loom...

What then of the social engineering projects?
Trials and testers of rare good idea perplex,
pushes and shoves of Ill-conceived unfair specs,
beyond all common reason or clear mind expects.

The ignorant brute of Red Devil SOB socialism,
thru eyes of Marx and Engels social science prism.
The thievery and sick debauchery of communism,
lying and cheating activism of absolute barbarism.

Those in control command reign of power,
in charge of public stage and human wage;
pseudo-intellects demanding from ivory tower –
rarely admit mistake, pull back pain, and disengage.

So then... what is the key?
The difference between science and ill-born sociology;
bravery to work for truth, and not for what evil eyes see;
the wisdom to start over, and not pursue crazy ideology?

Path to freedom begins in Veritas fair thought - -
genuine ways and rights of justice complete.
Do not accept ordered labor and sacrifice, all for
naught;
or believe decrepit ruler actions are sincere, while you
sleep replete.

Slate of nation must be clean from bottom to top.
Human spirit must have undying force of loyal
commission.
Leaders who bend must be made to unbend, or face
swap.
Start over, if need be, and send vile sinners to perdition...

Strong Man Son

Would evil exist on earth, if not for Man?
Animals more vicious than human clan?
Do packs of lion or fox maraud and fun kill?
Maybe Dog – friend of Man – perhaps still…

Trace of ungodly element in our genes,
hidden behind smiles and black screens.
Confuse advancement with jealous greed,
injecting in culture seed – murder creed.

Of unconscious brain stem survival reflex,
in curse hex union backbones of double helix -
errant pirate nucleotides with sharp sword…
Something wicked stored – the Mongol horde.

In frontal cortex, thought centers of mind –
one can find secret grind of vile unkind.
Nerve paths with treacherous interneurons -
misfire and misdirect dangerous liaisons.

It falls now on you – my 'Strong Man Son',
to fight the war at hand until it's won…
To secure surreal peace eternal that truly is,
and know in heart of hearts – ultimate bliss.

Proceed indeed, down untraveled road;
clutch tight liberty, never failing virtue code.
Realize impossible - human core without vice,
and ever forever achieve sacred life paradise…

If I Had Not Known You

If I had not known you...
would morning not broken,
or night not settled dark?
Would Truth have been unspoken,
or song unheard of meadowlark?

Would hover dance of bumblebee,
or flight of Monarch be absentee?
Would wind over calm sea not blow,
or rich green grass not further grow?

Would earth and star and moon stand still,
and all matter universe lose expansive will?
Would endless spinning top of Time stop,
or giant dream balloon of humanity pop?

NO

Yet, if I had not known you...
beauty of orange ball of fire dawn,
and cool spritz of black evening frost,
would all have been lost and gone -
as tender voice of songbird exhaust.

Color of bee and butterfly washed out;
flowers would not sprout alive and shout.
Ocean surf would not glisten silver white,
and verdant field would be lesser sight.

Heaven cosmic study would lose smooth spin,
as meter Time would tic and toc in ugly din.

'Bang of Big' would have no rhyme or reason,
and sanctity humanity would fade in depletion.

For, if I had not known you…
I would not feel the sweet velvet rose petal soft,
or see flare pure angel white snow mountain aloft.
I'd be unaware of fresh scent gardenia fair,
and sun's glare on your magnificent auburn hair.

I'd be in silent memory of most wondrous find,
of rare fantastic enchantment - one of a kind;
untouched by your lips sent from Almighty above,
and the charm and rapture of truest truelove…

Absence and Persistence

What is this feeling - - -
a revealing, or concealing?

Why is it, I hurt and want;
and also sense you inside,
and outside - - -
an alleviant so buoyant?

Why can I cry - and smile;
yet too, smile - and cry?
Is it a hostile sorrow bile,
or pleasant sigh - with no goodbye?

Mysteries of tender inner self,
so deep dark or lit light - - - -
Old fright tale on a hidden bookshelf,
or sweet love ballad reunite...

Mastery of the mind affect,
so difficult and facile - - - -
To work and fight to straight direct,
or let flow free and gracile...

Why in your absence,
do I feel your persistence?
In the longing,
so much belonging?

Could it be two are truly one,
like star and sun?
And a soul is dual,

like diamond is jewel?

That spirit ether can be all in all,
as black space in cosmic hall...
And your soul, and mine,
are caught and mixed - entwine...

So, when I miss your distinct presence,
and feel the sorrow tear so strong - -
I reach down for profound persistence,
remembering you've been with me all along...

The Night We Met

Living bold and strong,
without yet understanding...
I had learned all there was,
performed outstanding - -
Always ahead of the pack,
with measured advanced planning;
achieved the mind mountaintop,
obstacles notwithstanding...

As charged electron spin
around atomic nucleus,
jumping to higher orbit win –
tho dubious energy Vesuvius.

As searchlight thru Space,
at infinite spirited speed - -
No origin track, no early trace,
like wild stampede of steed.

The missense of 'knowing',
feeling aware of Time and Place.
Confident stand ever glowing,
on moving Earth grace base.

Then --- in the tropical night,
under flow of moon and star,
in veiled scent of orchid white,
with sound of piano and guitar.

The catch of eye, the look,
patting of lash and pout of lip,
the body moves while Earth shook,

beginnings of the hip courtship.

The saintly spicy smile on you,
with its beauty and saucy erotic…
The cobra tongue and cheek brew,
pure perfect breast and pelvic exotic…

Ultimate feminine knockout blow,
between my eyes and into heart.
Forgetting everything, and all I know;
first born blast, old life fall apart…

To imagine I had breath before our match,
a beating core and thinking mind…
To have felt I understood worldly catch,
life's deep maligned and bright shined…

To have known astute the smallest quantums,
workings of physical and chemical matter;
to have lived in my deepest psychic sanctums,
and now see thickest learned book in tatter…

On the night we met,
all before now forget;
with roar of love onset,
and Time of clock reset…

From real to magical surreal,
a dream without need of past;
a wondrous place of reveal ideal,
where all good true sensations last…

Grand Salvador

Awake and free in peace land of living;
green forest and silent stream flowing;
with flower color and songbird singing;
pastel sky bluest blue, and sun shining.

Home with a view, where our children grew;
surround of tender calm wind and gentle palm;
to where life pursue with you, and our love withdrew;
where not even atom bomb could still amor psalm...

Afloat in dream, cast away from social strife -
with you, my wife, in the most content life.
To believe forevermore that good things last,
and these feelings held fast are never in past...

In garden of red cardinal and soul carnival,
sounds of fountain waters in bright light.
Sight of hummingbird jewel worshipful,
and harmony flight of pair angel dove white...

Through all nature beauty splendor,
melody of your true voice comes to me.
I close my eyes, and in quiet surrender,
allow inside the marvel image of thee...

I see in mind, the eyes that drew me,
with their soulful love and magic serenity.
I see the mouth and lips that kissed mine,
with their sense so genuine, and taste divine...

I feel your hushed breath behind my ear,
and warm patter of your heart on chest;

I hear words of romance Shakespeare,
and endear soft music of tongue expressed...

I have so cherished – loving you,
embraced and adored ways true...
Feeling all of your kind spirit in me,
realizing our souls complete and free...

I will continue to live in nature of your,
form creation of our minds' peace outpour.
Close our doors, and sit by our shore;
breathe pure love airs of Grand Salvador...

On Your Birthday

On your birthday, there are things to say...
My wished words useless to convey,
but I will try to express feeling anyway –
before this special moment slips away...

I've had great joy of your essence:
calm serene pose and love presence,
your caring true ways and soul amaze,
sensuous energy and fire spirit blaze...

To have even known you...
Graced by your voice yet once,
sense your force break through,
see with my heart all beauty fronts...

For you and me to have been born,
and never met, lives never passed...
To have not looked into eyes adorn,
or not fallen into a dream so vast...

To have not pressed our lips firm,
and felt the blood rush from our core;
to not have shared in great transform,
or explored *amor* spout from every pore...

I thank dear Lord Creator for your birth,
to have been given splendor and glory.
For there is no one else on sacred earth,
to complete allegory for grand love story...

Act III

Air

In our journey search for perfect ideal – none such, in
reach for perfect utopic uniqueness and ultimate fit, in
great seek explore for the wonder of elegant dream - - -
we may find dystopic reality without refuge, without
secure peace comfort, without island...

Intangible ethereal journey from cortex to stem;
survive in mind, or physical duel in natural life fight;
select for consciousness or reflex, and struggle for them;
inspire breathe and metabolize, or reach for eternal light.

With each heavy mallet strike of all worn iron spike,
align of flesh and bone to wood, hoist on cross pike - -
Final end run with only one exit escape: free thought
flight.
I fade in waning daylight, and bring you to internal
eyesight.

If even once consider: expansive universe beyond hither,

the spread of atom matter past all - to ultimate giver.
Immense forces of nuclear nature into things greater,
to incredible wonders without known nomenclature.

In those intense dances of galaxy bodies,
the spins and whirls of suns and globes,
crashes of planet against planet binaries –
productions of secret mathematical codes...

Explosions of stars into heavy elements,
across a dark and open cosmic canvas;
spring of magic life molecule experiments,
in the blackness – light and life in all practice.

In cell, with special organelle: a symphony -
the nucleotide, to protein and polysaccharide.
Walls and membranes, in bioweb company -
stacks of life, and the complexity it can provide.

In natural selection, from simple to grand:
the birth of sight in deep oceans – to land;
development of primal nerve to encephalon,
from brain to conscious, and all its carry on.

Rise of Man, and amazing master plan -
with senses to taste and feel, vision to scan;
with kidney and liver to detox deliver,
a heart to pump blood oxygen caregiver.

Organ systems and their mighty functions,
not simply to provide seed of next generations -
but in the main, the brain and its constructions:
a loft of consciousness and its deliberations.

Could it be a splendid sacred decree,
that Man in all his grace and disgrace,
was made from star embrace and all that be –

to ponder and wonder of existence and his place?

That Man was born to think, and not to subsist -
to use his higher functions to synthesize and assist?
And if so, must not one be free to clearly think -
alive and unencumbered to dream and interlink?

And in our consciousness, if free to roam and fly –
do we not land like feather on the altar of love?
Where calm peace waits, in emotion high;
thoughts on a plateau above, and in all thereof...

So - in a very direct way, in life and all its ray -
from origin burst, into light of cosmic day -
we were born to wander construct in mind,
and somehow arrive at true love and all its find...

I have beached with wounds to isle;
to its white sand shores, blown alone.
No friends in welcome to spend the while,
no reservoir – as expected – in which to atone.

My presence of altered state,
with stream of thoughts jumbled.
A wait of unknown fate decimate,
of stumbled people crumbled.

Inflictions are of body and soul:
slow pool flow of blood from flesh,
and image conjures of mind not whole.
Yet, your remain imaginings – fresh.

Girl with black beret, and no name...
Knowing sure all we overcame,
living in world aflame in shame.
We gathered and survived – became...

I saw lights of atom and disease of germ,
darkened poison of sky and black rain,
rejection and burn of the weak and infirm.
Felt all losses human heart can contain.

But, how did we arrive at such vile contrive?
From what brains did these disasters fly?
Who made wrong decisions of error deprive?
Who showed the world emanations of evil eye?

The ruination of the delicate life symbiosis,
magic runnings of cell mitosis and meiosis,
the interlace and smart database of DNA...
All rejected by human race, and thrown away...

One can trip and fall in love with a girl,
and not even be aware and know her call.
Surround of given name is not the pearl -
but only true joy inside, for once and for all.

Here I am on 'Isle of Hope'...
Yet, where are you?
In my clouded mind vision myope –
your fine image real, and unreal too...

I am carried to tall treetop hill, above sea;
marine ribbons of wavy blue, of you and me.
Sharp displace of calm ocean from swirl sky,
rare violet purple and orange of soul supply.

Why the peace I sense, in such unsure display?
A tender sound in ear, in much lacking sun ray - -
Your voice calling to me – guiding me up path,
ridding heart of discomfort and painful wrath.

Further nail, driven hard and deep...
Tacked to rail, I sail in silent weep.
Many around, in loud cry and wail.
How much longer, this sad sad tale?

A howl wind blows cold...
What remains of grass green grows old.
My head nodded down in gravity,
in turns of wrongs and depravity.

What could have been done in change,
in strange range of great leaders' derange?
In the many hazard turns to left and right,
could people's plight been raised in fight?

Or are we, from simple womb embryo be,
already with stick and stone and dagger arrow,
to club the head and break the weak knee,
split the bone and steal the blood marrow?

Are we destined from first conception,
to compete and destroy with heart nurture?
Bedeviled in a gray black zone inception,
to search out all hurt and torture?

In my teachings of art and mathematics,
in number sequences and mixed colors,
in grand patterns of truth design statics,
I tried in best to reveal world's wonders...

I believed in opening eyes with beauty,
prying away sinister say with fine line.
It was my calling, my ultimate duty -
my grape and vine in the divine shine...

More iron into me, great pain to side.
Large wounds gape open wide.

There is a suffering to be had.
Where is the good in all this bad?

As far as the lights of my eyes,
in all directions as crow flies,
bodies rise...

Crosses of man and woman and child,
like rows of dead forest timber wood.
Too many to count, the numbers piled -
evidence of Man's mind misunderstood.

Frigid airs wrap and tear,
robbing heart of all care.
A wish to die,
in harsh crucify...

The night black as coal,
Heaven and Earth in death roll.
Colors sapped out whole,
in horrid vitriol...

Mourners around,
near piles surround.
Lamentations of innocents,
songs of dissonance...

I wish this girl with no name –
freedom, in a world tame;
a free expression of thought,
creative for great goods sought.

Internal drive for justice and liberty
cannot ever be stamped out.
Life rights and balanced equality
for progressive civism without doubt.

There is no way – no End or After War,
no atom bomb or pandemic abhor,
no sword slash or sharp knife in chest,
that can quell flame of bosom breast.

They can perform evil deeds to extreme,
scheme the worst to extinguish our dream.
Yet, we will remain steadfast – everlast;
and at close, we the people will outlast...

My mind has run off into oblivion...
Has all this been a sleeping illusion?
Am I to wake return, alive dynamic,
with open views of my lands panoramic?

Have the battles and sail of seas,
the girl with black beret and fine way,
been all a melt of subconscious ease,
or deep dream from a forgotten day?

The little life remaining, slips further;
pain gaining, I continue to fade...
Hands and feet tight, no preserver,
betrayed in my long lost crusade...

Below my post of crucifixion,
in midst of friends and foes -
those forgiven and unforgiven,
beneath flying raven and crows...

At last ---
The care face with red rose...
With hair free, and spirit too,
composed, coming up trail she chose.
Defiant she is, in the cold dark blue.

In thick black robe - she moves,
between crying mourners and enemy;
girl courageous, show of love proves.
In my loss, a final sacred gifted remedy...

She weeps, with hands on my torn feet,
never once removing eyes from mine.
Her wet orbs express love complete.
Treetop hill has become our shrine...

Beyond at great distance, sun starts its rise;
I see slight of light in her precious eyes.
Grand star introduces new day on new Earth,
and with new dawn perhaps, hope of rebirth.

'What is your name, Girl?' I ask silent.
'I regret your presence on this sick isle;
'I wish far more for your dear ardent,
'not this infernal fear and hurt compile.'

She peers into me with her unique strength,
wiping away her painful sadness and tears.
Pressing her lips against the sole of feet alength,
she softly sings a love melody of the spheres.

'What is your name, Girl?
'You must say... your name.
'In this new dawn, with my love unfurl,
'tell me your call of great dame.'

She looks up at me, and exclaims,
'We have troops in the faraway hills,
'strong and armed with weapon reclaims!
'They are young, but with great skills.

'We will win our holy freedom soon,

'and our people majesty in new moon.
'Have faith in me, and hope for your son,'
she whispers, pulling robe undone...

Wrapped to her, like cub to bear,
a baby boy --- asleep and fair.
My son... My son, with girl without name,
offspring of our great love aflame.

Hung on a wooden cross,
my eyes in teardrop gloss.
Steel with spite thru flesh,
muscles torn open fresh.
Beam of sun hot stone,
no lite wind has blown.
Like an effigy of terrible enmity,
surrounded in quiet elegy.
My fighting heartbeat,
in a struggle complete.

To have come to this ---
A total war born of culture divisions,
the many ill commissions,
the insane indecisions,
the imprecision of coarse mind visions...

And of our split nation youth, what comes?
To believe in a good Creator?
To trust again in future humanity sums?
To be ruled again by a human spirit traitor?

Will Man ever again put heart on stone,
sculpt deep love on grave and bone,
discover science in chalk or Petri dish,
measure number, or sing dear song wish?

I will not know...

I go now into soft wind blow.
From the sea – a steady light,
photon flow in calm transparent white.

Into an eternal sleep,
hallowed zone of existence deep.
Realm of ever love and kind peace,
where all pains cease…

'What is your name, Girl?' I ask again…
After dark night, now in bright of early day,
before my last short breath and pass away - -
In her loving strong hard way, she say…
'Ulyssia…'

'U,' I exhale…

Acknowledgements

As author of this narrative poem, I will forever praise Man's great desire need and passion for humanity, and forever struggle against his depraved falls into inhumanity.

www.ingramcontent.com/pod-product-compliance
Lightning Source LLC
Chambersburg PA
CBHW021124130626
46554CB00002B/860